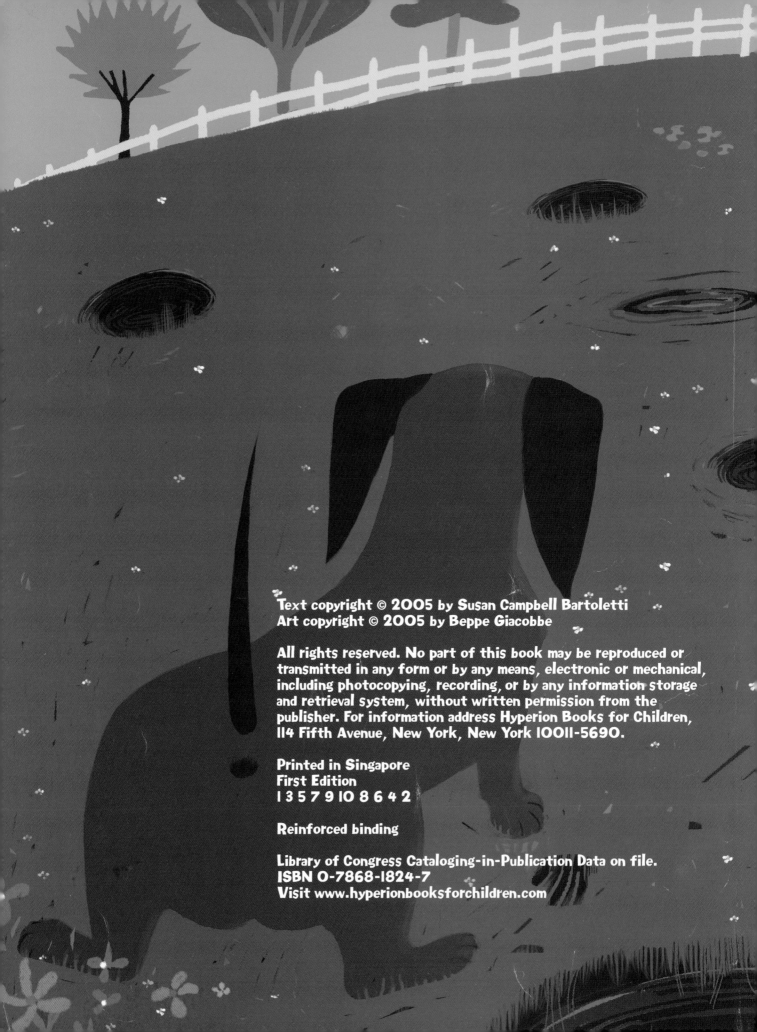

Printed in Singapore
First Edition
1 3 5 7 9 10 8 6 4 2

Reinforced binding

Library of Congress Cataloging-in-Publication Data on file.
ISBN 0-7868-1824-7
Visit www.hyperionbooksforchildren.com

To my son-in-law Rick
—S.C.B.

To Princi, Greystock, and Picasso
—B.G.

Nobody's Diggier Than a Dog

By Susan Campbell Bartoletti

Illustrated by Beppe Giacobbe

DOG CATCHER

Hyperion Books for Children   New York

Nobody's **DIGGIER**
than a dog—
a bury-the-bone dog,
a shake-a-paw dog.

Nobody's
PIGGIER
than a dog—
a dribble-drool,
toilet-drink,
breathy-stink dog.

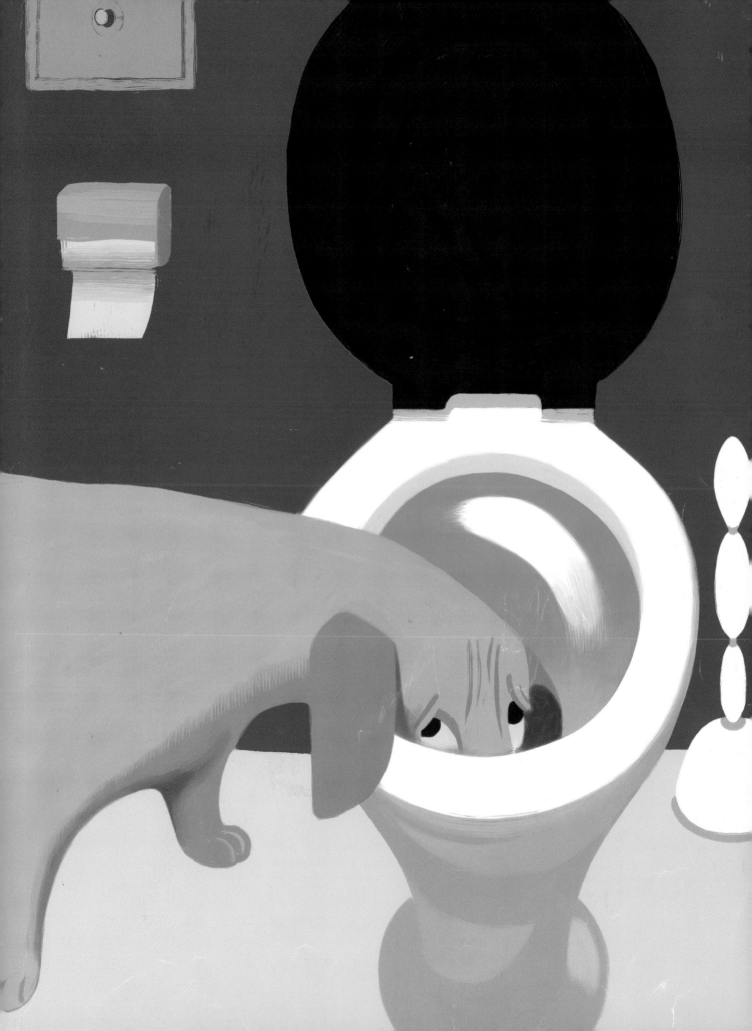

BEWARE OF DOG

Nobody's
MIGHTIER
than a dog—
a *ruff*-'n'-tumble dog,
a guard-the-yard dog.

Nobody's **FLIGHTIER** than a dog—

a thunder-crack, scaredy-cat,

run-and-hide dog.

Nobody's **NAGGIER** than a dog—

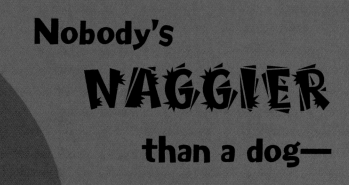

a slurp-your-face dog,
a let's-play-chase dog.

Nobody's WAGGIER than a dog—

a meet-'n'-greet,
belly-up,
rub-a-dub dog.

Nobody's
CRAZIER
than a dog—

a tailspin dog,
a wind-grin dog.

Nobody's *LAZIER* than a dog—
a choose-to-snooze, snore-on-floor,
total-bore dog.

Nobody's
SORRIER
than a dog—

a chew-the-shoe dog,
a *What'd-I-do?* dog.

Nobody's STARRIER
than a dog—

a nose-stuck-up, breeder's-cup, paws- . . . .for-applause dog.

Nobody's **SCRATCHIER** than a dog—

a *Let-me-in* dog,

a *Let-me-out* dog.

Nobody's **CATCHIER** than a dog—

a fetch-the-ball,

call-and-call,
stop-'n'-go dog.

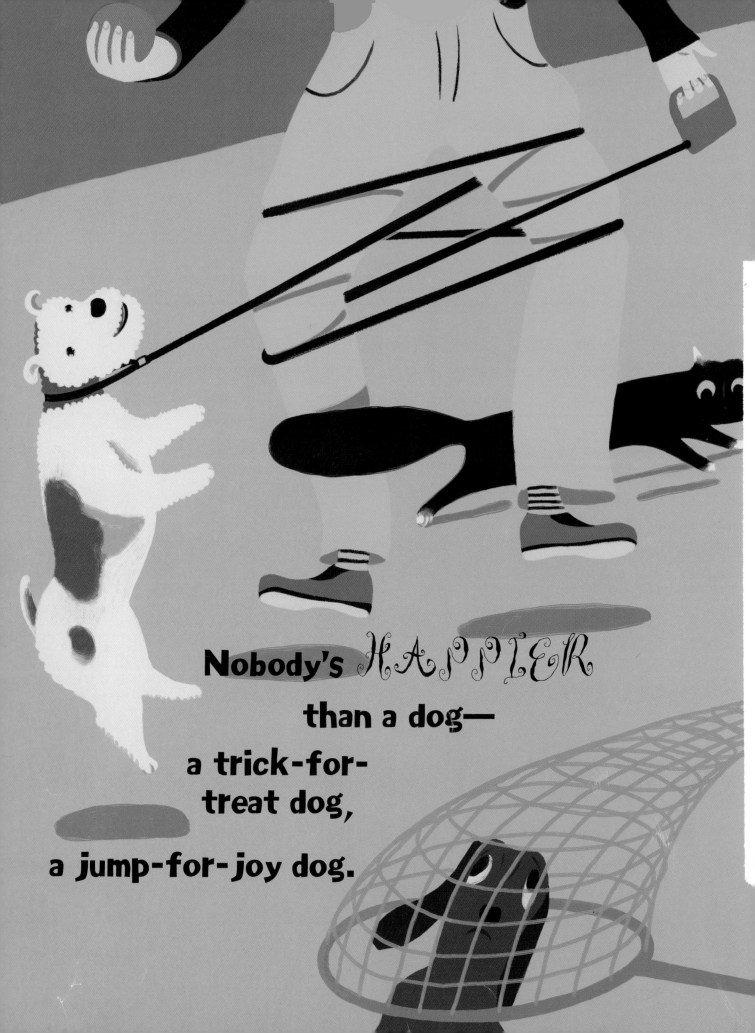

Nobody's *HAPPIER*
than a dog—
a trick-for-
treat dog,
a jump-for-joy dog.

Nobody's MUDDIER than a dog—
a romp-'n'-play dog,
a gone-all-day dog.

Nobody's BUDDIER
than a dog—

a big-bark, big-heart, brave-save dog.

MISSING

Nobody's **LEGGIER** than a dog—

a lift-the-limb dog,
a free-to-pee dog.

Nobody's BEGGIER than a dog—

a puppy-eyed, tail-tap, table-scrap dog.

MISSING

Nobody's
HAIRIER
than a dog—

a buff-'n'-puff dog,

a mop-the-floor dog.

Nobody's **SCARIER** than a dog— a lead-the-pack, take-no-flack, hackles-up dog.

Nobody's **PUDDLIER**
than a dog—
a swim-the-lake dog,

a shake-
shake-
shake-
dog.

Nobody's
CUDDLIER
than a dog—

a wraparound, lap-hugger,
bed-snuggler dog.
A lost-and-found,
dog-pound dog.

My dog.

11.05
3.05